JOURNEY TO MOUNT TAMALPAIS

BY THE SAME AUTHOR

MOONSHOTS (poetry), Beirut 1966.

FIVE SENSES FOR ONE DEATH (poetry), *The Smith, Ed.*, New York 1971.

"JEBU" SUIVI DE "L'EXPRESS BEYROUTH—ENFER" (poetry),
P. J. Oswald, Ed., Paris 1973

SITT MARIE-ROSE (novel), *Des Femmes, Ed.*, Paris, 1978; Beirut and
The Hague, 1979; Rome, 1980; *The Post-Apollo Press*,
Sausalito, California 1982.

L'APOCALYPSE ARABE (poetry), *Editions Papyrus*, Paris 1980.

PABLO NERUDA IS A BANANA TREE (poetry), *De Almeida*, Lisbon 1982.

FROM A TO Z (poetry), *The Post-Apollo Press*, Sausalito, California 1982.

THE INDIAN NEVER HAD A HORSE AND OTHER POEMS (poetry),
The Post-Apollo Press, Sausalito, California 1985.

ETEL ADNAN

JOURNEY TO MOUNT TAMALPAIS

AN ESSAY

DRAWINGS BY ETEL ADNAN

The Post-Apollo Press
35 Marie Street
Sausalito, California

Library of Congress Cataloguing in Publication Data

Adnan, Etel.
    Journey to Mount Tamalpais.

    1. Adnan, Etel—Biography. 2. Poets, American—
20th century—Biography.   I. Title.
PS3551.D65Z474   1986   811'.54 [B]   86-12228
ISBN: 0-942996-01-1

Simone Fattal, Publisher
The Post-Apollo Press
35 Marie Street
Sausalito, California 94965

Book Design by Simone Fattal
Composed by Michael Sykes at Archetype West
Point Reyes Station, California

Printed in the United States of America.

JOURNEY TO MOUNT TAMALPAIS

SOMETIMES, THEY OPEN A NEW HIGHWAY, AND LET IT ROLL, OPEN WIDE THE earth, shake trees from their roots. The Old Woman suffers once more. Birds leave the edges of the forest, abandon the highway. They go up to mountain tops and from the highest peaks they take in the widest landscapes, they even foresee the space age.

The condor is dying. He used to live on the top of Tamalpais. His square wings used to carry him all over the area: the hills were moving beneath him with silent pride. He used to cut through the clouds like a fearful knife. At certain seasons he used to carry the moon between his claws. Now we took over his purpose. We are the ones to go to the Mountain.

This morning I took the card table and put it out on the deck, under the pine trees. On a piece of paper shadows fell. I tried to catch their contours but they were slowly moving, all the time. They made me think of sidewalks on which people pass, swiftly. And the big mountain sent a wild smell of crushed herbs into the air making everything feel slightly off.

Like a chorus, the warm breeze had come all the way from Athens and Baghdad, to the Bay, by the Pacific Route, its longest journey. It is the energy of these winds that I used, when I came to these shores, obsessed, followed by my home-made furies, errynies, and such potent creatures. And I fell in love with the immense blue eyes of the Pacific: I saw its red algae, its blood-colored cliffs, its pulsating breath. The ocean led me to the mountain.

Once I was asked in front of a television camera: "Who is the most important person you ever met?" and I remember answering: "A mountain." I thus discovered that Tamalpais was at the very center of my being.

Year after year, coming down Grand Avenue in San Rafael, coming up from Monterey or Carmel, coming from the north and the Mendocino Coast, Tamalpais appeared as a constant point of reference, the way a desert traveler will see an oasis, not only for water, but as the very idea of home. In such cases geographic spots become spiritual concepts.

The pyramidal shape of the mountain reveals a perfect Intelligence within the universe. Sometimes its power to melt in mist reveals the infinite possibilities for matter to change its appearance.

I watch its colors: they always astonish me. When it is velvet green, friendly, with clear trails, people and animals are invited to climb, to walk, to breathe. When it is milky white it becomes the Indian goddess it used to be: a huge being with millions of eyes hidden beneath its skin, similar to the image of God I used to have in my childhood days. When it is purple, it radiates.

About three in the afternoon, the mountain starts to swell. The colors and the shadows sharpen. The volumes come into fullness. It all looks so mysterious.

The community sleeps at its feet and in the middle of its trees. Houses live in close friendship with redwoods, pines, and the tallest eucalyptus in the world. There is a smell of wilderness in a civilized county thanks to that majestic being which stands among us in all its beauty.

There is a monkey-tree in the garden. Its branches are monkey-arms opening into clusters of hands. Through them you can sense the purpleness of the mountain, far away, in all its power. Birds fly. They web their ways around the trees and they sing.

It was my destiny to join in a great experience: to live with the mountain and with a team, to encounter them regularly, to know them without ever reaching a point or an end, the way people know a river.

For years I am going, coming back, turning around the mountain, getting up in the middle of the night to make sure it is still there, staring at it, walking all over it, and dreaming, dreaming . . .

For years there has been an experiment going on at its very base: we are a team of people who gather somewhere in Mill Valley in peaceful parties with the seriousness of children at play. We are most of the time painting but this is beside the point; our involvement is with Perception. Ann O'Hanlon, who started it all, says: "To perceive is to be both objective and subjective. It is to be in the process of becoming one with whatever it is, while also becoming separated from it."

This living with a mountain and with people moving with all their senses open, like many radars, is a journey . . . melancholy at times: you perceive noise and dirt, poverty, and the loneliness of those who are blind to so many things . . . but miraculous most of the way. Somehow what I perceived most is Tamalpais. I am "making" the mountain as people make a painting.

TAMALPAIS THIS MORNING HAS MANY SHADOWS LIKE AN AFRICAN BEAST touched by dew. At its left side, at its base, light unfolds like a peacock's tail. It is lost amid clouds and says that heaven touches earth and that matter has an erotic substance. There is translucence in the great expanses of grey and there is the possibility for an angel to come across.

The month's name is autumn and it is melancholy. The mountain escaped everyone's attention because huge fires erupted all over Marin County. Mike's ranch is burning and his mother saw the furniture taken away and she

could not understand why. "Who is putting on all these lights?" she asked. They had to tell the children that grand'ma had a way of seeing all of her own. The heat went beyond 90 degrees. The summer is never ending, never. The mountain is hidden away by steam, not by fog.

It is rushing toward Kentfield and San Rafael. It is an animal risen from the sea. A sea-creature landed, earth-bound, earth-oriented, maddened by its solidity.

The world around has the darkness of battle-ships, leaveless trees are spearbearers, armor bearers, swords and pikes, the mountain looks at us with tears coming down its slopes.

O impermanence! What a lovely word and a sad feeling. What a fight with termination, with lives that fall into death like cliffs.

O Sundays which are like vessels in a storm, with nothing before and nothing after!

Standing on Mount Tamalpais I am in the rhythms of the world. Everything seems right as it is. I am in harmony with the stars, for the better or the worst. I know. I know. I know.

This morning it is springtime. The softness of the sky envelops the mountain with solicitude. Flowers come out and despair is held at bay. . . . Memories are as fresh as cool water and a cool breeze floats over one's fever. The pure blue of heaven is mixed to the clouds. The moment is accepted. The weightlessness of the air is all over.

The mountain slopes converge to the top as if for a tribal gathering. Up there, the open but filled mouth of the volcano speaks back to the sky a tale of past disorder. The fire has left for its own origins: it returned to the sun. The mountain remains in blue silence, in purple desertion, in agony, and nobody knows.

The ocean, below, beats, trying to reach the crater. Tamalpais looks over the hills, the rings of beaches, the screams of so many tempests, the sensuous futility of many storms, and the warm, agonizingly warm, insistence of so many suns. And Tamalpais remains alone, wise in its ingathering, peaceful in its knowledge, happy. Do not climb that mountain unless you know it needs you. Otherwise, you shall die like a diseased raven, and carry your skeleton in crowded streets, and never, never, recover your memory.

Tall trees of so many kinds, from redwoods to manzanitas, oaks, madrones, maples and elms, plants and bushes, flowers and seeds, acorns and grass, they all are the last chance of the earth and they all make a thick and permanent coat, a cover, a bath of perfume, a touch of healing, a royal procession, music and fanfare, they rise and talk to Tamalpais, and sing lullabyes and songs of love.

Only troubadours will save us. San Francisco is always there, outside the place in which we live. It is always like a former city, as if its inhabitants had left on a UFO for another planet. The city remained as a witness, a three-dimensional theater stage, a festive, decorated, luminous construction of the mind and of millions of hands.

On KPFA George Jackson is speaking. We hear a tape made while he was still alive and in prison. He has many voices blended in one, many accents. He cuts his sentences short, sounding like an Englishman. Then his voice slides between his lips, and his longest word, his most important one, the one pronounced with a long, burning, agonizing, pleading, and ever sure voice, is the word love.

The ocean is launching its brilliant waves against the asphalt-black walls of the mountain, and in the night of this ocean I am finding the freshness of dispersed springs. Harbors catch fire at the edge of the sea. Everything, at last, is upside down. The skies are confused with blackness and the water is green like eyes which are cruel and opened on smoke.

I feel trapped in this universe and think of what an anti-universe could mean, which is still a universe; there is no way out.

When the sun sets behind any mountain it looks as if some extraordinary things are happening, back there, in and beyond the sunlight. We want to be on the top of the mountain and see its other side, and further, knowing well, though, that other mountains, hills, or at last, the curvature of the earth itself, will always hide "whatever is going on there." And we are left with the sort of wonder that the sense of eternity always carries with it.

When the car turned down D Street, the mountain appeared like an Angel with a sword telling us to stop. We received it like a blow in the stomach. But everything being mobile like the earth and the sun, we eventually left Tamalpais behind, in its blue grandeur, its puzzled spirit.

Often, coming back from the Richmond Bridge, just when San Quentin is left behind, at a certain curve of the road, there surges an event, there happens a double movement: the lateral movement of the car, to my right, and the vertical movement of the mountain which seems to be rising from the ground. She seems to be rising and filling a configuration that I already know is hers. That's where comes, for me, that feeling of latent prophesy that I associate with the vision I have of the mountain.

Cruising on Magnolia Avenue, in Larkspur, we were chasing the clouds. They looked like flying saucers. One of them was Moby Dick itself, starting a new voyage in a new ocean. They were moving in slow circles. So was Tamalpais: slowly rotating as the road was curving. And our minds too were furry, velvety, soft and curvilinear, our minds were the soft skin of the mountain and its gradually ever changing shadows.

The Indian called the Mountain Tamal-Pa, "The One close to the Sea." The Spaniard called it Mal-Pais, "Bad Country"! The difference between the native and the conqueror is readable in these two different perceptions of the same reality. Let us be the Indian and let be! What is close to the sea shall

15

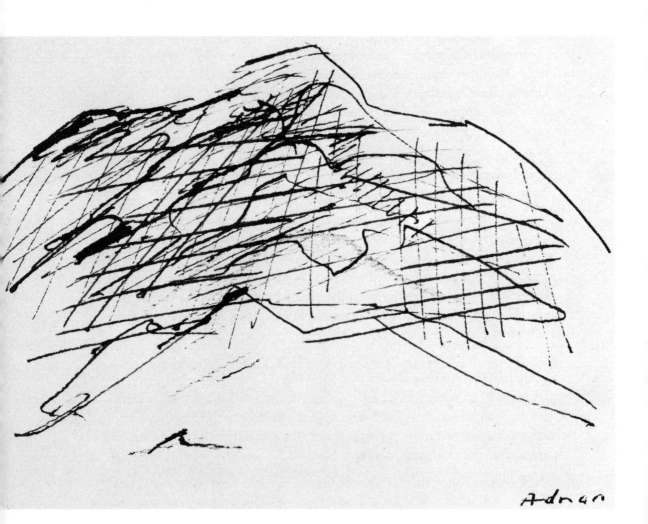

remain close to the sea.

This is, then, the place where the line is drawn. Tamalpais is the first of the mountains that constitute the convulsive spine of the American continent, all the way to Tierra del Fuego. It is the beginning of the chain of these green-coated mountains, guerilla-green mountains, green volcanoes, which give their fire and color to revolutions. Tamalpais is their peaceful kin. It is their starting point. Its peace is needed to understand the fire, for nothing can be outside a binary system. (And up north, with Mount Shasta, a new species of mountains develops itself, a different start.) It all is as if the equator of human destiny were foreign to the geological equator: the equator of human history is the latitude on which stands this Mountain that looks like an elephant and feeds on green grass.

I am at the window and Tamalpais looks back at me. I am in pain and it is not. But we are equals tonight.

I am sitting in front of that window as if I were in a movie house. The screen is miles away. Tamalpais is spread over it. I am watching a light-show. Clouds are moving in a peculiar way. I barely see them. All I see is the movement of a large beam of light which slides over the mountain, illuminating it gradually. It is all green, greyish green and bluish green, and the clusters of trees, like woollen balls, roll one after the other.

The large beam comes again. From the West to the East. The beam moves, revealing gradually and exclusively, places of its own choice. It goes on, it seems, for hours. I am amazed, but, more so, I am fulfilled. I am transported outside my ordinary self and into the world as it could be when no one watches.

The wind rises from the East. It is blowing toward the Ocean. The light-show reverses itself.

Tamalpais is jungle-green again. Light moves under and through the clouds. Almost horizontally. Like an army of irregulars. A big grey cloud passes over a huge white one: war and competition in the skies! Among the infinite varieties of blacks, whites, and greys, there are expanses of sulphuric blues. Tamalpais fumes. It is again a volcano.

I read in an old page of my Journals: "March 13th. 1967. Today, all the memories of the universe, as universe, and I, became one. In front of the Mountain."

To be: the light over there, breaking the clouds, alone in the cool winds, peaceful over the waves, knowing the mountain, and the ocean furiously possessed by its love for water. Drown and do not drown, the mountain is as solid as fog, as translucent as the undertow, as possessed as the ocean, but its travelling is silent and formal, and the ocean is a pure voyage.

A Voyage is like water. A pure experience. What kind of an experience? A JOURNEY. I am water and I move. I need to circle the mountain, because I am water. The mountain has to stay and I have to go, and it all comes to the same thing.

A RED DAWN RISES OVER THE BAY TO FOLLOW THE BRIGHTNESS OF THE SUNSET. I told the mountain: the ocean is sucking the tides and receding. I am flying but not moving. You are coming but disappearing.

I have been a boat wandering for long and when I came home the harbor was destroyed and I painted the sea.

The Pacific often sings a soft funeral march. It was most appropriate that they found a man hanging by a tree near the top of Tamalpais. It was not horrible. It was just one of the many events that happen up there following the death of birds or the growth of plants.

18

We need the mountain in order to be. Or to disappear. When we return from the Sierras we see it on the horizon and we know it is home. Its form is the substance of what we are. When I make a gesture, casually, I draw it in the air, without even realizing it.

WHEN I THOUGHT A BIRD WAS FLYING, IT WAS THE SOUND OF WATER. I thought a stream was running, it was the wind. Tamalpais became a space-ship ready to take off. Tamalpais is my space-ship.

The mountain is an animal wounded on its way to the sea, its limbs grasping the earth. I call it "The Woman."

"In the end," says Jung, "man is an event which cannot judge itself but for better or worse is left to the judgement of others." So the mountain looks at us. One day I withstood its judgement, and became one with it.

But, then, we also are bees. Running from storm to storm, carrying seeds from one perception to another. And once in a while the great rains come and everything is destroyed.

It had snowed. Tamalpais was white as it rarely is. White is the color of terror in this century: the great white mushroom, the white and radiating clouds, the White on White painting by Malevich, and that whiteness, most fearful, in the eyes of men.

Television is white, pale as God: an infinite amount of channels masterminding everything, projecting the ant-like destinies of us all. The mountain is its opposite: aloof, waiting for us to go to it, innocent.

It was a September evening. The moon had come out above Marin County, nearly full. Whatever her fate, she looked perennial. Cars were blindly running on the highway disturbing the Mountain, harassing the old giant.

We, members of the Perception Workshop, had climbed a steep trail thinking of rivers abolished, of a long travel across lava country, of sudden bursts of meteors. We had with us no rite of passage. We had gone through no initiation, as we went into childhood and into adolescence with no warning. This is why we come to the mountain. We have no other elevation.

We slept under trees but in fact within the mountain's vast sadness and we awoke very new.

The night freed us from our obsession with reason. It told us that we were a bundle of electric wires plugged into everything that came along. It was enough to be alive and around. The same was true of everything else.

The next day we moved around the upper part of the mountain. Tamalpais is for us what San Francisco Mountain in Arizona is for the Hopis: the mountain to whom messages come. After a long march we arrived at sunrise at the top. To Observation Point. Saw the land from Half Moon Bay to Tomales Bay and to Mt. Diablo. This walk was the new order: the search for perceptual ecstasy whose totem pole is a spider. At the center of the web is Tamalpais.

To the Indian, the Old Creator gave Thunder, a spirit power, and said to him: "Your spirit power will be discovered and will be brought back to earth to be of great use to the human race." And this spirit power has been discovered on this land, and it is Electricity, and it works as no magician ever thought.

This is the Navajo song of the sick man when he is sitting in the middle of the sand painting, waiting for the painting to absorb his sickness:

With good ness and beauty in all things
around me, I go.
With good ness and beauty, I follow immortality.
Thus being I, I go.

We are moving in our experiments toward the new sacredness of images, we are understanding images to be our equals, having a life and a power of their own. We make them but they are not ours. And they are not from us.

In the meantime, in Pennsylvania, a bird is trying to talk: a warbler is trying to send a message, like a prisoner pounding on a wall.

Forty-four percent of the children of the State of Virginia prefer their T.V. set to their father but prefer their mother to the T.V.! We talk about it in the seminar.

The radio says that the voyage to the moon is a hoax and that it had happened over the Nevada Desert. Did they forget that in the summer of 1969 the White Man went to the Moon and the Red Man to Alcatraz?

In front of the Buena Vista Cafe, in San Francisco, Jack Burlybum was selling jewelry made of Indian bones unearthed in a Northern California burial ground. The Indian sitting next to me by the sidewalk said: "They took our land and now they are selling my bones!"

I told him how the Bay was blue, and that Angel Island was dark brown, the color of live deer skin, and Tamalpais was as green as a crushed bottle of beer. . . . And he smiled. America, I told him, was torn between paradise and hell, and it was not suffering, it was numb.

Went to Santa Barbara. Drove east to Cachuma Lake. By the road, a narrow road, darkened by trees and underbrush, I found the Indian cave which has rock paintings. The little cave is like a cell with an iron gate. You have to look between the bars. I felt a woman in love with some prisoner. The paintings had the whites, dark browns, turquoise and blacks we are familiar with because of sand paintings and rugs. But there is so much more than color and line: they are depictions of high energies of the mind, things we call visions. We go into outer space with rockets. Some people in previous times went as far with the sheer power of their mind and the pureness of their heart. They used

"Nature" the way birds use air currents to fly. And they saw things our astronauts do not speak about.

Who is going today to the empty and haggard "City" to mourn the Indians? We are occupied by winter and the affairs of the Hemisphere, while, among many catastrophies, the Kurdish woman in Beirut carries her headless son through the streets. The human race, though, is a single tribe. Tamalpais is the head of the tribe.

I ALWAYS THOUGHT THAT DREAMING WAS THE HONOR OF THE HUMAN SPECIES. The logic of dreams is superior to the one we exercise while awake. In dreams the mind at last finds its courage: it dares what we do not dare. It also creates: from nightmares to fantastic calculations . . . and it perceives reality beyond our fuzzy interpretations. In dreams we swim and fly and we are not surprised.

For years, Tamalpais is speaking itself into dreams, telling about the past and the present, or, rather, transcending any notion of ordinary time.

One October night I dreamed that the whole mountain was made of glass, a thick, greenish glass, with long and rusty streaks of kelp within it. I was lying over it, looking in, and discovering Indians telling me with sign language and impatient gestures that they were imprisoned for centuries. There was nothing I could do to liberate them and cold sweat awoke me.

Dreams spill over on our days. For some people they never stop spilling: the visionaries, the hobos, and all those who speak to themselves, aloud, in the big cities.

In a roomful of dreams do not go. They will invade you and eat you. But if you are a painter, go in, they will be friendly. And look at the night: it is a reservoir of black ink you can use on virgin paper.

23

As I was walking, once more, I met a young woman sitting by a trail. We talked for a while. She told me that the ancestors of the human race had thrown the sun up in the air and that the universe reddened and burned slowly and devoured them . . . volcanoes threw up more suns and more moons (Tamalpais was one of them) and they are still burning somewhere, and that we are searching for them, astronauts are combing space and looking for them, and we shall one day find the hour, the place and the light.

I was sleeping. My eye lost its sight. For every crime, every murder, the moon bleeds and gets cut into halves and quarters and dark clouds sweep across the skies.

Tamalpais was spitting hot clouds. The Indian was away.

Between my eyelids moved a film-like thing which made my eyeball rubbery as if the moon with its craters was turning within my face.

The coming generations will go to the moon easily, to look at her sierras, her granite walls and powdery seas . . . they will feel her surface which is an underfired glaze, solid, porous, glass-like and powdery: I can see them sitting on that edge with their legs hanging in the void . . . and then they will carry their shadow to other planets.

Two strangers visited a dream, again, an early morning dream: they wore clothes like F.B.I. agents but they were creatures from outer space. They looked familiar but felt utterly different.

I had a dream which was of a passage between Hell and Paradise: when one is happy this river-passage flows upstream. When one is sterile, it flows down towards Hell. But then, sometimes, one swims in a direction opposite the current, the river goes to Paradise, the swimmer to the bottom: that is the process of creation.

I would like heaven to be a place where I can go and talk to Paul Klee. To-gether we will look at circles and see dots in them and in the dots we will discover universes and we would visit within them all the houses he has painted.

The Iroquois had a single divinity: the dream. We waste ours . . . but a long walk on the mountain often brings them back, they come back like three dimensional movies, they roll with the hills.

I know of experiences which happen only on some special elevations. Patrick Shields was a Pawnee Indian. He had been back from the Korean War and only one day later they found him in San Francisco in a flea-bag and shook him out of a drunken sleep to tell him that he had beaten a woman nearly to death. There was some doubt about the testimony of witnesses. All he replied was: "If you say I did it I must have done it." He got 12 years in San Quentin. One day he walked away from the prison and swam across the wintry mud flats of the Bay to Corte Madera, then went to Tamalpais. Three days later he came down, entered the first house he saw and surrendered. When I asked him what the mountain had told him he replied: "She told me that it was not the woman that I had killed, it was America."

Sometimes, while painting, something wild gets unleashed. Something of the process of dreams recurs . . . but with a special kind of violence: a painting is like a territory. All kinds of things happen within its boundary, equal to the discoveries of the murders or the creations we have in the world outside.

We translate our dreams on paper and cloth, subduing them, most of the time, fearing that moment of truth which has energy enough to blow up the world. In a painting you may be bringing down an angel. In a dream I climbed the 3000 feet of Tamalpais in a matter of seconds.

The mountain stands blue, erased by streaks of clouds, visited by rain, slippery to all hands.

I looked at the linden trees of Grand Avenue and they were feeling as cold as I. Tamalpais also was shivering. The month of December was stretching towards its end.

A bird ran into the glass door of my deck and died. I rushed with paper and a pencil to make a drawing and realized I couldn't draw death. The record player was playing a Koranic prayer recorded in Tunisia. The lamenting voice of the Prophet became a funeral song for the silenced animal. I came in and saw my Ray Bradbury book opened on these lines:

Robins will wear their feathery fire
whistling their whims on a low fence-wire
and not one will know of the war, not one
will care at last when it is done. . . .

Through the long night of the species we go on, somehow blindly, and we give a name to our need for a breakthrough: we call it the Angel, or call it Art, or call it the Mountain.

PAINTERS HAVE A KNOWLEDGE WHICH GOES BEYOND WORDS. THEY ARE WHERE musicians are. When someone blows the saxophone the sky is made of copper. When you make a watercolor you know how it feels to be the sea lying early in the day in the proximity of light.

Painters have always experienced the oneness of things. They are aware that there is interference and intervention between the world and ourselves. One day the sun participated in our workshop: it hit suddenly the nose of a cone on a bronze wall sculpture made by Dick O'Hanlon. It was while we were speaking of the sun of Ancient Egypt and Akhnaton's solar monotheism. We were saying how underground a deity was the sun, immersed in moving waters, dripping, trembling, subversive, young. . . . Dick has always had a passion for astronomical charts, sundials, civilizations expressed in pyramids, stones, and calculations. . . . He was contrasting the liquid deity which presides over Pharaonic thinking with the sun of geometry, severe, charted, pure, equally mysterious in its simplicity.

Whatever one's feelings, the moment of painting is always a moment of happiness. The rape of materials is a joy. To break, squeeze, manipulate, transform, build, open, force, make . . . all this is a sport and is a moment of love. Hell will belong to the folklore of the past, and suffering will feel monstrous, out of place, if we say paradise now, and use our hands.

A community of artists is like a community of bees . . . a small whirl, flying around each other in circles, they gradually rise into the air, the bees, with their old queen flying along with them, and like Sufis they want to reclaim the body's former powers and its inbuilt knowledge. The queen bee, emerging from her cell as a virgin, must first achieve her marriage flight. . . . And why do I think of Emily Brönte when I remember that a queen is never fertilized inside her hive? She takes to the air to unite with a drone high up in the skies. It is this marriage in mid-air, be it with a person or a form, or some material, that makes the moment of perception to be a moment of art.

It is with an eye that does not belong to the sea that one paints.

When Alexis Leonov returning from outer space declared that he saw more colors in space than on earth I realized that the object of our search is these other colors, related to the arts of fire, born out of the blackness of outer space, the blackness which has swallowed what we called spirits, daemons, and the early birds. The youth around us, in workshops, classes, trails . . . is breathing fire and bringing down the altitude of the skies. Each one of us is alone in that effort of creation as if, each person, to itself, were the resume of all.

In these years, in the O'Hanlon workshops, by the small town of Mill Valley, and the Mountain, within that triangle, we tried to paint and think about painting. We tried to find value to the process of seeing and translating it on some surface. Painting and perception formed an unbreakable dual concept. They became interchangeable.

I noted down some fleeting trajectories of thoughts, questions, intuitions, of inner and outer events, noted things as they came. There is no system to Perception. Its randomness is its secret:

· The Beginning made movement, movement made the sign, the sign made the planets, the planets made the forms. The forms made themselves.

· Lucretius says of men that "they chose the sky to be the home and head-quarters of the gods because it is through the sky that the moon is seen to tread its cyclic course with day and night, and night's ominous constellations, its flying torches and the soaring flames of the firmament, clouds and sun and rain, snow and wind, lightning and hail, the sudden thunder clash and the long drawn intimidating rumble." He makes us breathe again.

· There is a new sun, everyday, a ball of fire, which is independent from the sun.

· Clouds cut into the moon and burn her substance and she is reborn, but tied to her path, regaining her light, and crumbling again.

· The sun and the moon are the same thing. The moon and the sea are the same thing. The sea and the sun are the same thing.

· Painting landscapes is creating cosmic events. The actual space of a painting—its very dimensions—is the space of memory. When our eyes are closed, the widest fields occupy a screen of a few inches. We paint that screen on a canvas which, in its turn, refers our memory back to the world at large.

· I think night is a black cloud that enters space as a fog then comes as ink on virgin paper and then returns to the infinite sky.

· Youth is that sense of depth, of space, of distance, of seeing things from always a far-away place, a past we call the future. It is this distance which shrinks, along the years, and we feel closer, more equal to the people in history, but also impoverished, abandoned by grace, moving away from the divine, that which used to be called the Center.

Could a painting find that early space, at least once?

· There was a Frenchman who was an adventurer. He went to Iraq and told the people in the middle of their hottest summer: "Sublimate your pigments-color into light color . . . resuscitate the form out of the line. Exorcise the shadows . . . as you did in the XIII Century."

· The peacock's feathers contain no blue pigment, but a regular scaly pattern adjusted to blue light.

· Our century is a boat many want to leave: some went to the moon, others are going into the past, looking for ancestors, ruins, records, measurements, fossils, photographic plates of past events. . . . But we don't need to move. To perceive is to be the movement, not the object.

· "Why does the eye see a thing more clearly in dreams than the imagination when awake," asks Leonardo.

· Reason is but another form of magic. Anthropologists will soon study "rational man," his systems, his myths, his constructs, everything that reinforces the sovereignty of consciousness over innocence and reinforces the nightmare. Let's go to the Rain Forest!

· I was walking at night on leaves not yet dry but yellow and fallen, and crossed the street at Belle Avenue and Grand, and turned suddenly, and felt that I had left something of me behind, like a snake's skin, and looked back and could almost see myself, being there, standing . . .

· It seems to me that I write what I see, paint what I am.

· But autumn is marvelous. The trees, the small ones, are getting red; the taller ones are gold and yellow, and already, some are orange dry. No news from distant affections, no words to tell me if I am accepted or have been rejected, for ever. Tonight, the hills of the county are being cut and tamed and devastated, but the moon looks untouchable, a pool of nocturnal light in which some of us, later, will drown.

Whenever the mind sees, thinks, listens . . . it sees an absolute with which it confronts its perceptions. But with the moon, the absolute I create is equal to what I see. She is at her own level, queen of Matter, queen of Light, modern empress of our drives.

Looking at her perfect circle I realize that imagination always thinks in terms of the Possible. Pure Geometry is also pure reality. The Impossible is impossible.

· And there is you: like the mountain visited, battered, conquered, unyielding, constantly throwing every effort against a tangential line which opens up to infinity.

· The square is the passion of the circle.

· Jim told me that Paul Klee would have liked making drawings on the accordion-like Japanese books made of rice paper that I used for so many years. I like the flow, the apparent lack of boundaries, the river image of these long unfolding papers. China and Japan understood long ago that one reads an image the way one reads lines made of words. The rest of the world is slowly catching up with it. As for Paul Klee, our "master," the way Novalis had been his, his drawings are mountains regardless of their subject matter. They move counter to gravity, and every dot is pulled toward some edge which is not the frame but far beyond that, somewhere behind the sky, and his lines and shapes move in all directions, feeling the pulls, crucifixions, temptations of speed and direction, that a spatial world imprints on us. And there is also, in the same time, on the surface of his works, a strange and quiet breathing, like an early morning in a purely abstracted world.

· Something fell, splattered into pieces, the old alliance of sun and moon broke up: in the loft there was nobody but a tape of Ali Akhbar Khan playing music.

· Got up this morning after many nightmares, with the feeling that nowadays some people feel that they are expendable. They see art as casual, transient, ephemeral. But it is this quality that things have of shifting, this fast beauty, pervading some works whose purpose is to disappear behind their own power, this perception of pure light, this dissolution into ultimate evanescence, that makes the modern world as powerful as anything that has ever been. The only thing which is close to the Pyramids are laser beams. In the end.

· Poetry, it is believed, is the revelation of the self. Painting, the revelation of the world. But it could also be the other way around.

· Would a circle drawn on a piece of paper describe the reduction of the solar system, or the reduction of a human destiny? Who knows?

· Each time I draw a circle I draw the earth, the moon, or the sun. We see simple things. But the South Sea Islanders see in that very circle a mythological crab which has just emerged into the visible part of the globe. We have sterilized our visions. We need a new start.

· Nietzsche says that "around the hero everything becomes tragedy. Around the semi-god everything becomes dance." We could add that around Painting everything becomes Light.

· Vision is the fainting of the eye on the object. Perception is a laser beam which destroys in order to assimilate, it is an exchange of energies.

· In one of the early space experiments, three astronauts died in their spaceship which had caught fire. They died a claustrophobic death trying to open up Space. We painters do the same thing. Our works end up sometimes in some incinerated adventure: they take off with pride and temerity and only succeed to shrink to nothingness.

· Often I feel that we are alien creatures bruising Mother Earth, eating her plants, smashing her grass, fighting her clouds with our fists, raising her children for tomorrow's young wars. "Be as peaceful as I am," says Tamalpais.

· When Chou En Lai's ashes were buried in Peking his funeral appeared on television as dark shadows making patterns similar to Japanese Zen gardens. I was sitting in the O'Hanlons' house, in Mill Valley, where the Orient was introduced to some of us, where it was made as clear as it is.

· But here also, on Tamalpais' top, there is dust. The ground bones of the Indians, the echo of their obscure chants, the footsteps of their warriors. . . . There was a gaudy bicentennial and the Queen of England was coming. That is already dust. Hard to breathe. The past looks simply as a blanket, to most of us.

· I made a movie, once, of fog, fog, fog. They said: "It's a study in greys, an abstract movie, a joke!" It's none of these things. It is the fog.

· I draw roses. What if I do nothing but draw roses? Why not? Maybe at the end one of them will start talking to me. Will tell me unheard, undreamed stories, like how it feels to be under rains, to grow up in a garden, to be face to face with the sky, to have thorns and unbearably beautiful scents, to be strong and short lived, to come through life without making a fuss about it? What if a rose bush walked toward me and took me into its affection?

· Oh how I envied space walks, under cosmic rays, in waterless oceans, in uninterrupted curvatures, in pure flotation!

· To enter a house, once or twice, in a lifetime, with the feeling of entering someone's soul, to be close to some other identity than one's own, and then,

maybe, draw a circle on another circle, draw a horse, call the wind to the rescue.

· When you realize you are mortal you also realize the tremendousness of the future. You fall in love with a Time you will never perceive.

THE CAR IS PARKED BY A CURVE ON MOUNT TAMALPAIS. ANN AND I ARE LOOK-ing south at the Bay meandering through the hills. The radio is on. We are listening to Berg's Sonata number one. Ann's attention is turned some-times inward, filled with the music, and then she extends the look of her blue eyes to the horizon. It's a clear December morning: the clarity of high passes through the mountains. She recalls her campings on the High Sierras. Her in-tensity is rushing to its own fulfillment. While it lasts it looks miraculous.

The early workshops participated of the newness of the world. Yes, they were at the very beginning of the Sixties, yes, they participated in the pro-phetic spirit of a decade which has its equals in History in the Pre-Socratics, or, closer to us, in the decade which preceded the Russian Revolution and was made by Malevich, Tatlin, Kandinsky. . . . This time a whole nation was again being involved in a Great Experiment, unabashedly, through street marches, music, songs, underground movies, and millions of silent events which tried to uproot a culture and plant a new one, a new forest. The workshops in Mill Valley found, at least for a handful of us, their place between Castaneda's Yaqui Teachings, the powers and winds and visitations of the world, and Mao's people, the Chinese awakening for a new morning, on the other side of the Pacific.

There were fun moments, by the thousand. Laughing in company is the greatest pleasure. Saying meaningless things which fuse out of the mind with the speed of lightning is a moment of great communication. (Like the day someone said while everybody seemed to be trying to concentrate on some activity: "9th and Euclid is the coldest corner of the United States!" She was expressing, we learned later, her homesickness for Cleveland, Ohio!)

I can't say we had privileged moments. Life per se appeared as a privilege. We didn't need more. The O'Hanlon house was in itself a living poem. I stayed once in it for a couple of weeks, while they were away. In December. The air was crisp, I looked into the sky for hours through the windows. Space looked with no orientation, as it should. It was wilderness. The young tree by the bedroom opened up overnight like a Japanese umbrella. Pine trees were climbing a pyramidal hill. They were on an outing. Huge birds were chasing each other with no hurry. The horizon was extremely high. It was practically a vertical plane. One night I slept in the living room under a square skylight. In the middle of the night I got up suddenly. The moon was above me like a dagger. I woke up many times that night. In the morning Simone told me: "I saw the moonlight on you and did not want to wake you up. The moon did walk on your head!" The pointed roof made a window on trees as high as hills.

BETWEEN THE SUN AND THE MOON, THE RESTLESS DESIRE TO LIVE AND THE restless desire to die, the mountain holds the balance. Tamalpais spins the seasons and stands still.

Going up Throckmorton Avenue, it resembles Ramses II of Egypt or, perhaps, the Sphinx. Silenced volcano, with a few stones still running out of its mouth, it pulls the tides. On its top, standing, one wants to keep going, out into space, alone, bombarded by all the travelling particles that exist.

From their very beginnings, we followed the space travels of America, from the Mountain. Ann, Dick, John Humphrey and I spent hours, days, years in front of the television screen. We tried to figure out the color of outer space, the speed of the rockets, the landscapes seen by the astronauts, their thoughts, their feelings, their mutations.

Tamalpais is a space-launch and the Tamal Indians knew it: they are still living on it, transformed into trees. Some of them are madrones, others are oaks. The Old Creator had told them: "Your spirit power will be discovered and will be brought back to earth to be of great use to the human race. The power to soar."

I will always remember the day Ranger 8 hit the moon. It was a Saturday, in February. It sent back the first close-ups of the craters and of a face which was pocked, rubbery, like burning milk breaking up in bubbles, and stretching its skin. We felt like we were sitting within that strange lunar smile making fun of earth-bound creatures.

On the same television program appeared Red China's first nuclear explosion and I saw not only a mushroom-like form, but a human brain. It was like the birth of the human brain under our very eyes.

Then Tamalpais appeared on that screen: clean, singular, triangular, Buckminster Fuller's primeval form: a tetrahedron.

Ranger 9 took off from Cape Kennedy and from the television set. Its rocket spat fire. Moments later we saw two roundish spots of light and a flow of fire looking like a gigantic white beard. When I was 9 years old I had seen that beard in a dream, that waterfall of pure energy under a semblance of a face, and I had thought that I had seen God. I believed then in what I saw.

And if you like numbers, I will tell you that here on earth it was February 14th, and it was spring: flowers were all around and a warm breeze was mixing my fever with the clouds.

Thus, we moved irrevocably toward man's first landing on the moon. I drew lunar sunrises but it was futile. Television was overpowering. We saw Neil Armstrong put his feet on the moon.

Then, incredibly, the news switched to the faces of some young Vietnamese convicts who were freed and used by the U.S. Army as infiltrators. There was an ugly happiness on their faces, a determination to stay alive at any cost, that sent shivers along my spine. Isn't perception always redefining Evil?

It snowed on Tamalpais. The news went around. It was unusual for the Mountain to be suddenly so white. My friend Bobby came. He said: "There is a visitation from above." Snow on the sacred mountain. We decided to go out.

Snow is cold, as cold as the Indian buried underground. And still, the Indian was everywhere in the fog, totally a spirit.

We walked down to Stinson Beach and Bolinas. The tide was low. We walked for miles. The water looked wet like streaming metal. All kinds of brittle blue streams were moving between flat rocks. I was in a car accident and dying. It seemed like it. Bobby found at the same moment, in a tiny pool, a small, silver-clean, dead fish. I realized that my death had been transferred to the fish. I was safe for awhile. The same night I was, in my sleep, in the Paris metro. Funerals were coming in that underground corridor, a black hearse leading. I moved then to an empty apartment. Looking down the stairs I saw the funeral procession coming up. I took the elevator down. There was a woman in it, I kissed her and realized her face was covered with tears. A sense of compassion pervaded the whole space.

The next day was filled with cool air and a metallic light and we decided to look for the oyster-boats in Point Reyes. Bobby had worked on them. It started to rain very hard.

We waited for the night, but the rain got fierce. We went. The night was even more beautiful: thick with patches of blackness streaked with water. Under the automobile lights the water was sizzling on the ground, sputtering noisily, pounding the road. The storm had the power of a forest of trees breaking down simultaneously.

Bobby's truck had a broken window on my side. The wind was rushing the rain in. On his side, the door was broken and held with a rope knotted to his knee. His speedometer was out of order. So we charted our way out by following the red lights of the cars ahead. We were roaring with laughter. Sliding, swerving, loosing sight of the red beacons ahead, watching the curves, going fast, once in awhile unsticking the windshields, we were as wet as the mountain and as free as astronauts. In fact, freer. The highway was our sky. We made it to the boats. They were empty and shivering in the storm.

Later in the week, we went back, back to the mountain. The snow had melted in some spots. We found an inscription (as if the snow had pulled aside to make it visible). Somebody had written: "I spent the time making vast toothpick cities for the future based upon the rainbow." We spent the afternoon repeating this sentence. We walked through the cities of the poet, talking to their inhabitants, as if we were on a trip from Marrakech to the Andes.

We were surrounded by running springs. The skies cleared. We stopped here and there, overwhelmed by their clarity. It was a deluge with no rains. The mountain was a water system. Waterfalls were cascading, streams were drawing watery lines. We came down, as they did, in the hush, tumble, dripping, running, of all the waters. On the floor of the valley we took roads which were lined with rows of linden trees quivering in a liquid gold tinted and interrupted by patches of green moss and the silver caused by the clouds. There was a young rainbow.

Our minds started to work like rakes, combing memories among the dead leaves. Bobby wondered how Kepler felt when he saw that the earth was a

magnet and the stars were suns, how his friend Mel felt when he went to see *Don Juan in Hell* played by an all-male cast in San Quentin, and the director of the theater told him that he was an artist in residence, a "lifer."

That night Bobby left for Canada. He was to take a train. In the dream that followed I was a camera and my face a big lens. I was surrounded by White Whales burning at their seams, as if they were both alive and gigantic toys. They had a sneer while flames were seen in transparency behind their eyes and like spouts were coming off their heads.

To EACH PLACE, THERE IS A COUNTER-PLACE, LIKE THE SECOND PLATE OF scales. Ours is Yosemite Valley.

Yosemite clears the soul and takes all sorts of cobwebs away. For the members of the workshop it has been an open book: perceptions are enhanced, refreshed, brought to some real perspective. It is there that we see shadows as solid as granite, trees reproducing the contours of clouds, the solid grounds of eternity giving meaning to our transiency.

Looking at the waterfalls, in May or June, one remembers, or rather sees perfectly, Leonardo da Vinci's renderings of the deluge. In northern Italy the visionary Leonardo has noticed the structure of wild water, the laws that govern matter under its most fluid form. The drawings in the Windsor collection made by the ageing genius, of water observed at the foot of the Alps, of nature in delirium, could also have been the best rendering of Yosemite under water. Yosemite is an ultimate space.

The Valley could also be Dante's Paradisio. Stars fly over Yosemite like airplanes, and trees stand by their own free will. They stretch in the purity of the air and keep company to the valley.

We often went to Tenaya Lake. If one is desirous to understand Plato one has to go there and sit and look at the lake and let it tell you what it is: a pool of light different from ordinary light. The energy that pushes mountains upward, stones into wells, people all over the globe, seems to come to rest in Tenaya Lake, gathering itself so that it could go elsewhere and move the world.

A PAINTER ALWAYS LOOKS LIKE A LONER. HIS WORK SEEMS TO BE THE RESULT of a solitary struggle. Many painters could envy the collaborative arts, the musicians, the singers. . . .

But one day at the Loft we broke tradition. An extraordinary thing happened. Ann distributed huge pieces of strong paper, most of them around seven feet by seven. Somebody started painting on one corner, someone else took another corner, and a third party came into the picture and within an hour or two there were five or six people working on the same surface, overlapping, interfering with each other's work, as dancers will do when improvising.

For weeks, the group painting went on. The results were remarkable. They proved a point which matters in contemporary art: that a group of artists can make a painting together, the way jazz musicians work.

The collective paintings had, each, more quality, more strength, more "unity" of composition and feeling, than many individual works. They were exhibited in the Cannery, in San Francisco, and they looked astounding. Each one of them said a single, although mysterious, thing. They looked at the public with certitude, the way the mountain looks at us: their thereness could not be put into question. Through them, a moment, a group, an adventure, a culture, found its expression. They were a being made of us all.

Shortly after, the O'Hanlons left for a 64-day bus journey which took them from London to Calcutta. Ann had painted a very large Buddha. When she realized that the members of the seminars were 64 in number, like the 64 chapters of the *I Ching* which she often consulted, she cut the Buddha in as many pieces, and decided that on her trip she would send each day to one of us a piece of the canvas. A particular town or place had to correspond in her mind to the person who was going to receive that day's mailed piece. And that's what she did. It was understood from the beginning that when the O'Hanlons returned the pieces of the Buddha would be reassembled and the painting reconstructed. The travellers returned, but the Buddha remained scattered. Like us. Whatever is destroyed should enter, in order to be meaningful, other emerging entities.

I AM SITTING AS USUAL IN FRONT OF MOUNT TAMALPAIS. I CAN'T GET OVER ITS deep greens.

It is clear. It is empty. My spirit is anguished by color. Color is the sign of the existence of life. I feel like believing, being in a state of pure belief, of affirmation. I exist because I see colors. Sometimes, at other moments, it is as if I didn't exist, when colors seem foreign, unreachable, impregnable fortresses. But there is no possession of color, only the acceptance of its reality. And if there is no possibility for the possession of color, there is no possession at all. Of whatever it is.

Clouds come into the garden. They are lighter than the air. The wind blows while they float.

A pink smoke sweeps the sky from the West to the East. It is the evening fire, the one which leaves no ashes. The sun is far and low, as if absent, but light is fringed with fire and the mountain is of a new translucent grey.

Tamalpais is there, pale and fused with the ocean, with the Bay, with lakes and reservoirs. My right eye merges with colors. The other gets lost in infinity. We are not apples and oranges to be cut in two: we are binary systems yearning to transcend place and time.

The field of my memory is crossed by my photographer friend who lives high, under one of the mountain's peaks: he has been accepted into the realm of flowers and plants. He is working on a garden made of wild species. He loves their names and scents as much as their sturdy presence: zigadine, mahonia, indian warrior, sage, crawling manzanita with bell-like tiny flowers blooming in December . . . the wild garden becomes a moving patch on the floor of the forest, the trees seem to welcome their wide-eyed visitors, to bend and fret, to gain vigor. No camera penetrates this sowed kingdom, no wind disturbs this new turn of events.

Now the clouds are grandiose and turbulent. An autumn storm is coming. Whatever makes mountains rise, and us, with them, makes colors restless and ecstatic. At my right, the Tiburon hills are somberly yellow. They have a strange power in their color. Is this pale gold on the surface of these hills so extraneous to its own place, that it makes my mind jump into the notion of some past I never knew and which, still, strangely, I relate to them? Otherwise why should these dark and light hues of yellowish metal make me think of Louis the XIVth, of one of his incursions into Europe, of a particular hour and day of his life, that remains lingering between the known and the unknown, that I see clearly and at the same time cannot pinpoint and give as precise reference?

Do colors have the power to break the Time barrier, and carry us into outer spaces, not only those made of miles and distances, but those of the accumulated experiences of life since its beginning or unbeginning?

THERE IS A PARTICULAR EMOTION CREATED BY DAYS WHERE AN AUTUMN STILL moving into winter meets the first signs of a spring well in advance of its assigned schedule. These days are most puzzling and they bring to any journey, as short as it is, a sense of beauty which mesmerizes and keeps our tracks within boundaries which thus become not limitations but the frontiers of a land never exhausted.

In such days leaves fall as young men in war, softly, carrying a lingering life around them. They die dancing. It is a kind of an Indian summer particularly Californian. Roads find their way between hills burnt with dark brownish colors and invaded by a green dew. The first leaves of grass are the first signs of the upcoming seasons. There is no possibility to arrest for even a fraction of a second the movement of the surfaces of such bodies of water as Tomales Bay or Bolinas Lagoon. The pendulum of these aquatic regions is animated. Under the sunshine they look laminated by some live creature we call the Weather. That creature awakens our senses and makes us tremble like birds near a pond. The changes which are coming from far in the horizon are felt by the gardener the way they are felt by the blue jay who is eating nearby. It is not by our eyes that we are most linked to the rest of the animated universe, but by these inner stirrings made to capture the first signs of atmospheric changes.

So who can paint the weather? Turner came closest. But he apprehended it with his eyes and his intelligence, and sometimes, with that inner sense specialized in those inner weather reports that the soul carries about itself and which seldom reach anything outside the body.

I make paintings and watercolors of Tamalpais. Again and again. Why do I insist? Am I trying to hold some image, to capture some meaning, to assert its presence, to measure myself to its timelessness, to fight, or to accept?

I think often of Cezanne and Hokusai, of their relation to their mountain, and of mine. I know by experience, by now, that no subject matter, after a while, remains just a subject matter, but becomes a matter of life and death, our sanity resolved by visual means. Sanity is our power of perception kept focused. And it is an open ended endeavor.

But can I ever understand what Cezanne says in Mont Sainte-Victoire, and Hokusai in Mount Fuji, if, after thirty years, I don't know what Tamalpais means to me beyond the sketches, paintings and writings that involved me with her. I know that the process of painting and writing gives me the implicit certitude, carries the implicit certitude of what the Mountain is and of what I see: I perceive a nature proper to her while I work.

Tamalpais has an autonomy of being. So does a drawing of it. But they are mysteriously related.

A visual expression belongs to an order of understanding which bypasses word-language. We have in us autonomous languages for autonomous perceptions. We should not waste time in trying ordinary understanding. We should not worry, either. There is no rest in any kind of perception. The fluidity of the mind is of the same family as the fluidity of being. Sometimes they coincide sharply. We call that a revelation. When it involves a privileged "object," like a particular mountain, we call it an illumination.

Let us return to Cezanne. He is a petrol lamp. His glance lightens the things it touches. A sense of the tragic is always in the quality of a painter's glance, in the moment of choice, in the phenomenon called vision. Cezanne

was in love not with the mountain (or the gardener, or the apples) but with the moment when his glance settled on them differently than when he was promenading or was involved in a conversation. A painter's glance is bitter, in the sense Rimbaud gave this word. That's why this glance seems to erase the very object that creates its intensity, the cause of its intensity. ("To abolish . . . ," Mallarme used to say.) Cezanne turns light into an impersonal and cruel prism. And if we so much like his watercolors, it is because they escape our direct glance, they slide like mercury under our eyes, because there is between them and us an invisible obstacle which is both transparent and irreducible. It can lead you to insanity.

Cezanne and Dürer: Cezanne makes his inner landscape while going along the real one: there is a sense of perfect coincidence between the two. There is movement and suspension. With Dürer, the emotion felt because of the sheer beauty of his watercolor is doubled by the perception of Dürer's own emotion in front of the landscape that he chose to paint. Dürer is desperately close to his subject. This "double" emotion is also the key to German Romanticism.

To see in order to paint. To paint in order to see. Cezanne moves within this circle. With no satisfaction, no resting point.

Bobby said: "Cezanne is a Newtonian machine thrown into an Einsteinian space." Yes, Nietzsche also: his nine summers in Sils Maria were nine ascensions into the next century. Not a single soul saw the shape of his ideas because he was a mountain surrounded by fog, and everybody around him was earth-bound, he was a peak visited by a clarity coming from the sun and invisible from below. Mountains are transitions. They are impatient spaceships. Cezanne knows it. His works start with a calm perspective and then, Space-bound, attain the velocity of light.

RICHARD O'HANLON DIED AFTER THE SUMMER SOLSTICE OF 1985. THE SUMMER solstice happens to be Ann's birthday and it has also been Dick's favorite feast day. There was every year a celebration: huge barbecues on a deck protected by tall and practically luminous trees, lunches on the grounds of their four acres of California land, conversations under the shade of cabin-like structures, evocations of slide shows and field trips to far away monuments and museum's in Japan, China, or Egypt . . . that is always a cosmic day.

Dick died in his sleep, in the deep of the night. His spirit did not. It rather became more transparent to people who knew him. We have a sense of being closer to his work and to the meaning of his passage on earth. He had to disappear for people to acknowledge the special quality of his vitality. Since he is no more in his usual ways among us, life became something we hold to be more fragile than we knew but also dearer to us all.

The latest event related to his activities as a sculptor happened in Walnut Creek. There was a large sculpture show in a gallery and in its adjacent park. Dick displayed a huge work in black granite. He called it Meridiana.

It was dark, rather twilight, things were visible the way silver shines in obscurity. Walking in the park I stopped in front of a huge standing piece of sculpture: the granite was black and polished. It is a monumental piece the like of which I had only seen once in Baghdad, and that is the Babylonian stela on which the Hammurabi code was carved 4000 years ago. Dick's piece stood high and large. A few feet from the ground I saw slits, vertical slits, which suddenly changed the whole meaning of what I was seeing. I was in front of a time-table, a solar clock, and the huge granite which slightly curved in at the top, like metal sensors would do, became a musical instrument for giants, the hour-keeper for the new age. Seldom have I felt in front of a contemporary work the type of awe one feels in front of the Acropolis. . . . But here I did. Every great work in History points to outer space and we did not know it. Dick had said his last terrestrial word.

A few days before the night at Walnut Creek, I had the occasion of looking carefully at one of Ann's latest paintings: it is a large canvas on which Ann created the new space we live in. She did the counterpart of the granite work: hers also belongs to that aspect of the present age that will dominate the future. It is not a tri-dimensional space, it is the space of a sphere, a volume seen from the inside, because the further "out" we will go, the further "in" we will find ourselves. That painting says where we are going.

From another front line, news from the universe is pouring in. Voyager 2 has already travelled 2 billion miles and is sending streams of images from Uranus and its moons. It will go another billion miles to Nepture, it will go. We are well engaged into the outer frontiers. And further on, when we will go beyond the reaches of Space and Time, something else will open up, we will know what it means for the human species to become an Angel.

"Mount Tamalpais. 4 p.m."

Adnan

Tamalpais is the stem of the balance. There is a meadow north of the county, burrowed into the hills and the trees, totally turned toward the Mountain. One day while I was walking with a friend we both stopped and looked: Tamalpais was sliding. It was a big sail and it was going. . . . The eucalyptus, which make a tall forest all around, were marching, faithful army of the county. Tamalpais had posted her guards and they were following her. We discovered that the trees were walking trees. We told each other: "Let's keep it a secret. People will be scared if we told them what we know."

Each woman is a mountain. I remember those barren hills, ochre, yellow, amber-like, dry and crissing under the feet, quivering on warm nights, shrieking pain in summers of sunlike violence. I remember orange-colored mountains worshipped silently by dissident tribes. I remember plateaus fornicating with wind and dust, burning with desire, exploding in volcanoes under earthly malediction. I remember that mountains are women.

In this unending universe Tamalpais is a miraculous thing, the miracle of matter itself: something we can single out, the pyramid of our own identity. We are, because it is stable and it is ever changing. Our identity is the series of the mountain's becomings, our peace is its stubborn existence.